Tea FOR Ruby

by
SARAH FERGUSON
THE DUCHESS OF YORK

illustrated by
ROBIN PREISS GLASSER

A Paula Wiseman Book
Simon & Schuster Books for Young Readers
New York   London   Toronto   Sydney

To Beatrice and Eugenie—
you make my world complete
—S. F.

For Jacqueline Preiss Weitzman—
my sister, my partner, my friend
—R. P. G.

SIMON & SCHUSTER BOOKS FOR YOUNG READERS • An imprint of Simon & Schuster Children's Publishing Division • 1230 Avenue of the Americas, New York, New York 10020 • Text copyright © 2008 by Sarah Ferguson, The Duchess of York • Illustrations copyright © 2008 by Robin Preiss Glasser • All rights reserved, including the right of reproduction in whole or in part in any form. • SIMON & SCHUSTER BOOKS FOR YOUNG READERS is a trademark of Simon & Schuster, Inc. • Book design by Dan Potash • The text for this book is set in Fiddlestix. • The illustrations for this book are rendered in ink, watercolor, and colored pencil. • Manufactured in China • 1109 PXA 10 9 8 7 6 5 4 3 2 1
Library of Congress Cataloging-in-Publication Data • York, Sarah Mountbatten-Windsor, Duchess of, 1959– • Tea for Ruby / Sarah Ferguson, The Duchess of York ; illustrated by Robin Preiss Glasser. — 1st ed. • p. cm. • "A Paula Wiseman book." • Summary: As Ruby tells everyone about her invitation for tea with the Queen, family and friends remind her about how she should conduct herself. • ISBN-13: 978-1-4424-0743-5 (hardcover : alk. paper) ISBN-10: 1-4169-5419-8 (hardcover : alk. paper) • [1. Etiquette–Fiction. 2. Kings, queens, rulers, etc.–Fiction. 3. Afternoon teas–Fiction.] I. Preiss-Glasser, Robin, ill. II. Title. • PZ7.Y823Te 2008 • [E]–dc22 • 2007045350

You are invited
to have tea with
The Queen
on Sunday.

Please bring your very best manners.

"The Queen."

"The Queen."

The Queen."

"I've been invited to have tea with the Queen!"

"Ruby, I hope you will dress appropriately when you have tea with . . . "

the Queen"

OOPS

"I've been invited to have tea with the Queen!"

"Ruby, I hope you won't talk when you shouldn't when you have tea with . . .

"The Queen."

"I've been invited to have tea with the Queen!"

"Ruby, I hope you will remember to welcome people when you have tea with . . .

The Queen.

"Ruby, I hope you won't talk with your mouth full and won't tip your chair back and will use your fork and napkin when you have tea with . . .

the Queen."

"Tomorrow I'm having
tea with the Queen!"

"Ruby, I hope you'll remember to sit up
straight when you have tea with the Queen."

Today's the day!

"Let's hurry so we won't be late!"

"GRANDMA?"

"May I offer you more tea, Princess Ruby?"

"Oh, yes, please, Grandma. Thank you."